The Little
Stranger

MORMON GIRLS

SOPHIE, A KIRTLAND GIRL

Something Lost, Something Gained
The Giving Heart
The Angels Sing

HANNAH, A MISSOURI GIRL

New Friends
A Lesson Learned
The Little Stranger

Mormon Girls

HANNAH, A MISSOURI GIRL

BOOK SIX

The Little Stranger

SUSAN EVANS MCCLOUD
Artwork by Jessica Mormann Chopelas

BOOKCRAFT
Salt Lake City, Utah

Library of Congress Catalog Card Number: 96-86443
ISBN 1-57008-284-7

First Printing, 1996

Printed in the United States of America

For my first grandson,
Dylan Huff,
who also writes, draws
pictures, and dreams

The author and the artist acknowledge with pleasure and gratitude the invaluable assistance of Dr. Carma DeJong Anderson, who gave countless hours of counsel and instruction, and made available her wide library of resources and the even more impressive resource of her own knowledge and love of historical costume and design to assist this work.

CONTENTS

Chapter
One

THE STRANGER
APPEARS

Hannah brushed the loose dirt off the front of her dress and stretched her back. "My wagon is half-full already," she cried to her friends.

Sophie looked up and smiled. "You work fast. My mother would like you."

"Hannah does everything fast—she is the cleverest girl in our school," Lydia said, coming up beside them.

Hannah smiled back. It made her happy to think of how Lydia had become her friend. It made her happy to be here in her father's field picking squash and pumpkins with the autumn sun warm on her head. The November air was crisp with the fragrance of crushed leaves and ripe fruit. Above the girls, blackbirds circled, their cries sharp and lonely, their glossy wings shining green and purple in the glint of the sun. Hannah had invited her best friend, Sally, to come with her to the field, then had decided to ask Lydia and Sophie, the girl from Kirtland, if they would like to come, too.

"Your mother's got her hands full, and the boys and I have no time to spare," Hannah's father had explained. "But it would be a crime to let that food rot in the fields while people go hungry."

Hannah agreed. Every little bit was needed now, for the mob had trampled and destroyed many of the crops the Saints had been depending upon to get through the winter.

Hannah shuddered to think of that last day of October—Halloween day—when the Prophet Joseph and others had been taken away by the angry men who wanted to kill them.

God will not allow it, her father had told her. *It is not time yet for the Prophet to die.*

Their family had huddled most of three days and three nights in the cellar, hiding from the

mobs who were looking for Mormon men to whip and Mormon farms to spoil.

Heavenly Father will be with us, no matter what happens, her father had assured them. *He will protect us—or he will help us to bear whatever may come.*

Perhaps because their homestead had stood outside the city, the brutal men had largely overlooked them—their house, barns, and fields had remained unharmed. The first thing they had done when the danger was over was kneel down in prayer.

Now we must help others, Mother had said softly. *There are so many of the Saints who need help.* Her eyes had filled with tears as she had spoken. Father had leaned over and kissed her, then drawn her into his arms.

So it was that Hannah and her friends were in the field gathering vegetables for the widows and needy. A cloud passed over the sun, and the chill in the air deepened as Hannah bent to her work again. Suddenly she heard a shriek that sent prickles along her skin. She looked up to see Sally stumbling through the field, her pigtails flying and her face drained of color.

"What is it?" Hannah demanded as Sally came close.

"There's someone in the old barn!" Sally said, her voice a hoarse whisper. "I heard him—and I saw a shadow of someone moving inside."

Something in Hannah froze. "We'd better go," she said slowly. "We'd better get out of here now."

"It can't be a mobber," Lydia said, voicing the fear they all felt, "or else he'd have come out here by now."

"Not necessarily," Sally argued. "He could have been taking a nap."

"There could be more than one of them," Sophie added.

"Did you see any horses?" Lydia questioned.

Sally shook her head.

"Their horses would be inside," Sophie reminded them. "Where it is warm and protected."

Hannah felt fear tightening her throat and making her head throb. "Let's leave as quickly as we can."

"And as quietly?" Lydia asked, looking over her shoulder at the rusty wagons.

Sally put her hand to her mouth. "We have to go right past the barn," she gasped. "It's the only way out."

"Well, we're not leaving the squash here,"

Hannah announced firmly. "Not after all our work."

The girls agreed. "Let's say a prayer," Sophie suggested.

They knelt on the rough, uneven surface, and Hannah said a prayer, trying to remember the words Father used that always made her feel warm inside. Then they rose and began to walk out of the field, single file, pulling the creaking, rattling little wagons behind them.

As they drew near to the decayed, broken-down barn, Hannah felt a sense of panic rise within her. Every nerve in her body was tightened, and she was ready to run at the first sound. Then it came—a loud, scratchy noise followed by a series of thumps that grew louder and louder. Hannah's knees froze. She stood staring stupidly ahead, watching the gaping black hole, where the boards were warped and broken, that led into the barn. Then the noises came to a sudden stop, and a moment later they saw a figure emerge out of the shadows—first the head poking through, then the entire person, standing silent and blinking in front of them.

Chapter Two

SISTER WILLIAMS

The stranger had hair as black as the crows circling overhead and eyes as blue as the sky. His clothes were rumpled and soiled, there were streaks of dirt on his cheeks where he had brushed his tears away with dirty hands, and one thumb was stuck firmly in his little mouth.

"He cannot be more than three years old," Hannah whispered.

"Do you think he is not alone, then—that there may be others inside?" Lydia asked.

Hannah knelt down beside the boy, but he backed away a little. "What's your name, honey?" she asked.

"If anyone can get him to talk, Hannah can," Sally whispered. "She knows her way around boys."

But the little fellow did not budge or reply to any of their questions.

After hollering a time or two, the girls finally entered the great, dark cavern of the barn to take a look around. Hannah noticed that their young friend followed them, his hand still securely in his mouth.

"It's filthy in here," Lydia complained, scowling into the darkness. "I don't think there's a soul around."

She was right. After feeling their way as far as they could, and gazing up into the rafters, they decided the place was so empty and so filled with holes that it could hold nothing interesting. "I don't think even a ghost would stay here," Sally sighed as they found their way out to the light.

"Who could he be?" Sophie mused. "Do you suppose he is just lost, or . . ."

She did not need to complete the sentence; each had been wondering the same thing.

Sally's eyes grew wide. "What if his parents have . . . have . . ." She stammered a little.

"Let's take him with us," Lydia suggested, "while we make our rounds of deliveries. Perhaps someone will know him."

The child seemed pleased to sit in Hannah's wagon with the golden pumpkins and the green and yellow squash piled around him. Father had given Hannah a list of widows he wished her to visit. "Give to anyone else you can think of," he had added, "or anyone you happen to run across."

It did not seem long before the small wagons were half-empty and lighter to pull. Many of the houses where they stopped showed signs of the mob: windows broken and doors hacked to pieces, gardens trampled or burned.

Yet the women who came out to receive them and their offerings seemed always so kind and gracious. Hannah could hear no anger in their voices, nor see any bitterness in their eyes.

The women of the Church have the hearts of angels and the patience of Job, she remembered her mother saying after the terrible nightmare of fear and danger had passed.

Surely God is mindful of the sisters' sacrifice and their faith, Father had agreed. *We men try hard to look brave, but we would be lost without you and your courageous example.*

They showed their little boy to each woman they met and asked if she knew him, but no one did. No one had any idea who the silent child with the brilliant blue eyes could be.

At last the wagons were nearly empty, and the children were heading toward Hannah's house, where there was shade and rest and cold buttermilk waiting. At the end of one of the far city streets stood a tumbledown shack. It was set far back from the road, crouched and hiding, it seemed, behind tall pine trees that stood close together, like bristly green sentinels. At the very end of the yard an oak tree spread wide, trailing branches, as if to ward all visitors off.

"Let's hurry," Sally said. "This house always scares me."

"Like the barn?" Lydia teased.

"Who lives here?" Sophie asked.

"A witch, I suspect," Sally muttered.

Hannah shrugged her shoulders. "Nobody knows."

"Least we don't," Lydia added.

"Let's stop," Sophie said. "We have a few squash left and one good-sized pumpkin—"

The girls all stared at her. "Not for the moon would I go near that place," Sally shuddered.

Sophie smiled. She was remembering a wild night of wind and rain, and a mean old man she was deathly afraid of. "Wait for me," she pleaded. "I'll just be a minute."

"She's gone out of her mind!" Sally whispered as they watched Sophie disappear into the damp shadows beneath the pine branches. They listened. They heard her knock on the thin door; they heard the hinges squeak open—then the sound of voices.

"Do you think we ought to go after her?" Hannah asked.

Both Sally and Lydia shook their heads. The little lost boy sat sucking his thumb contentedly, his blue eyes never moving from Hannah's face.

"She's coming!" Sally breathed. And it was true. They could see the swishing colors of Sophie's apron moving along the walk. But someone else was with her—someone with a faded brown dress and gray hair, and a terrible limp that twisted her body into awkward shapes when she tried to walk.

"Girls," Sophie called out, "this is Sister Williams. She wants to take a look at Isaac."

"Is that the child's name?"

Hannah stared in amazement; the old woman's voice was as sweet as brook water gurgling over warm stones.

"No," Sophie smiled. She was remembering Isaac Porter. She had thought she hated him, but then he became her best friend. "I'm only calling him Isaac for now," she explained.

Sister Williams nodded, and Hannah hurried to pull the wagon closer to her so that she could look at the little boy more easily.

"Pretty child, isn't he?" she murmured. "Poor motherless thing." She spoke the words softly, though Isaac seemed not to understand them. Then she lowered her voice even further. "I believe I know whose child he is. But I must make certain." She reached out with a hand that was bent with arthritis and horribly wrinkled. With gentle fingers she stroked the child's cheek. "Would you like me to keep him for the night?"

This was too much for Hannah. "No!" she said quickly. "I'd like him to come home with me. I have lots of brothers, so . . . so . . . we'll know how to take care of him."

"Wonderful, my dear!" Sister Williams replied in her musical voice. "He needs all the tenderness and love he can get." She stroked Isaac's soft cheek again.

When she had straightened herself she thanked the girls for their gifts. Hannah felt so ashamed when the old lady said, "I was wondering what I'd cook up for supper tonight. God bless you for coming to my aid, girls."

As they continued homeward, Hannah was silent. *How often has Mother told me that fear shuts out love?* she thought, angry with herself for forgetting her father's admonition to offer help to any they came upon who happened to be in need.

As they approached her house she saw Mother sitting beneath the shade of her elm tree, a pile of mending in her lap. Hannah felt entirely exhausted, but she moved close to Sophie and, catching her eye, said shyly, "Thank you for caring enough to stop back there."

Sophie smiled sweetly and reached for her hand. "Don't be hard on yourself, Hannah," she said. "I learned my lesson with an old man I thought was ugly and hateful." Her eyes took on a fond, faraway look as she remembered. "But I was lucky. He decided to be my friend and stand up for me when I was frightened and in danger. He turned out to be kind and understanding and, I suppose, one of the best friends I'll ever have."

Hannah squeezed Sophie's hand before she dropped it. Mother caught sight of them and started waving, and Hannah forgot her weariness in the excitement of telling her mother the incredible adventures of their day.

Chapter
Three

FINDING OUT
ABOUT ISAAC

Mother did not hesitate; Hannah knew she wouldn't. She let her sewing drop to the ground and drew Isaac into her arms. His little black head rested against her shoulder as she stroked his hair and cooed to him—the way only mothers can.

"Poor wee lad, poor wee lad. Where are your mother and father?" Her eyes were moist and troubled, and even when the girls brought food to Isaac, she continued to hold him carefully on her lap.

Hannah walked with her friends to the edge of the yard to say good-bye. Soot, her pet goose, followed her, scolding noisily because he had not been allowed to come along for the fun.

"Hush!" she told him. "I have to think, Soot, and you are not helping at all."

He made low rumbling sounds the rest of the way back to the elm tree, where Hannah's mother sat with Isaac, but Hannah paid no heed to him. What in the world was she to do? *A child is not like a pet,* she reasoned. *I cannot go up to Mother and beg to keep him, as I would with a new kitten—as I did with Soot after he misbehaved.*

She worried back and forth, back and forth, but no ideas came to her. So, when she reached the elm tree, she dropped down on her knees and cradled her head in her mother's lap. "What will become of Isaac?" she asked, afraid to look up and see her mother's answer in her eyes.

"I cannot say right now," Mother replied softly. "Only Heavenly Father knows that. This child is in his hands—as we all are, my Hannah."

Hannah felt Mother's strong, capable fingers move gently over her head.

"But what if . . . He needs somewhere . . . Surely we won't . . ." She did not know how much to hazard.

"Of course he has a home with us, my dear, for as long as he needs."

Hannah sighed in relief and relaxed against Mother's soft skirts. The exhausted little boy had fallen asleep. He looked even smaller and more helpless lying limp and motionless in Mother's arms.

"I'll sew for you," Hannah offered, raising her head. "That is, until Isaac wakes up."

"That's the fairest offer you've made in a long while," Mother replied, her eyes twinkling. "I accept, and thank you."

Hannah offered a little prayer as she took up Mother's sewing. *Please let it be for a long while, Heavenly Father. Please let Isaac stay here with us.*

Then she nearly laughed out loud at herself. Another brother! What madness to even think of wanting one more noisy boy thundering about the house!

Isaac was like a sleepy little kitten, curled under a quilt at the foot of Mother's bed. He refused to wake up—even when Father and the four boys stood in a huddle staring down at him. Nathaniel began to poke him with a curious finger, so Mother shooed them all out.

Over dinner Hannah told the menfolk what had happened—all about the little lost boy who wandered out of the barn, and the witch woman with the voice of a girl, and the reason why Sophie had called the little orphan boy Isaac.

"Isaac it shall be, then," Father said solemnly, and Hannah wondered what he was thinking.

She could almost see the wheels of his mind turning quietly and surely behind his eyes.

When Hannah came into the kitchen the next morning she found Isaac sitting in the middle of the floor with Soot squatting beside him. They were sharing the same bowl of oatmeal—the child as noisy with his spoon and fingers as the big goose was with his bill. Isaac smiled at Hannah as she scooped up the bowl and shook a scolding finger at Soot.

"Isaac," she said, pointing at him. "Isaac," she repeated. He nodded, his little face intent. *What is his real name?* Hannah wondered. *I wish he could remember.*

When Father came in from his chores he bolted his breakfast down quickly. "I've an errand to run, Hannah," he explained between mouthfuls. "A few things to deliver, and some supplies to pick up at the mill. Why don't you ride along, and we can stop at—what is her name?—Sister Williams's house."

Hannah felt her stomach tighten and go weak, but she nodded. They must find out some time, and she would rather be there when they did.

As she jolted along in the big wagon with Father, she remembered how dusty and tired she and her friends had been yesterday, walking by

foot and pulling their heavy loads behind. But the faces of the women and the little children who had watched them bring their gifts—that had been worth every blister and every step!

Walking with Father up the dim narrow path, strewn with a layer of soft pine needles, did not seem so frightening, somehow, as Hannah remembered. When Sister Williams opened the door a smile softened the contours of her face and made her appear almost pretty.

"Come inside," she urged them. "I fear I've a sad tale to tell."

"Is it Isaac?" Hannah asked as she sat down on one of the old lady's three chairs and accepted the drink of cool water she gave her.

"It appears your little lost boy belonged to a young couple who were homesteading not far from here."

"Were they Mormons?" Hannah could feel the tight concern in her father's voice as he asked the question.

"Actually, no. Though, in a way, it was the mobbers who got to them. The woman died giving birth to another child, and the infant died, too."

Hannah caught her breath, trying not to picture such a tragedy in her mind.

"There were other children besides Isaac," Sister Williams continued. "One morning the father went into town for supplies and returned in the evening to find his house in a shambles and one of his children wounded by a mobber's bullet. The remaining daughter was unharmed. But his little son—Isaac—was nowhere to be found."

"Do you think the mobbers might have taken him with them?" Hannah asked, her heart pounding.

"The young father believed so—or that his small son was dead. After nearly a week of frantic searching, he packed up what remained of his family and left." Sister Williams sighed, and there was such tender sorrow in the sound that Hannah felt her very heart would melt into tears.

"Does anyone know where he headed?" Father asked.

Sister Williams shook her head. "'I'm getting as far away from this place as I can'—that is the only thing anyone heard him say," she replied.

Poor man, Hannah thought. *Poor little Isaac, frightened and homeless.* "Do you think the mobbers really had him for a while, or did he just wander off on his own?" she asked.

"I believe someone took the child, or surely the search would have uncovered him," the old lady replied. "'Tis a strange tale indeed. But truth has a way of being more twisted and turned than the most fantastic story might be."

"Could we find Isaac's father?" Hannah asked, her heart in her throat.

"I greatly doubt it," her father replied. "If we had even an idea of what direction he had taken we might have a chance. But now . . ."

The three sat silent for a moment.

"What will happen to Isaac?" Hannah ventured at last.

"We shall keep him, at least for the time being," Father said. Hannah felt as if a little of the weight had lifted from her shoulders at those words, and the warmth with which he spoke them.

"We'll be back," Father promised as they waved good-bye to Widow Williams.

"I'm glad I had an extra chicken and some of your mother's tomatoes to spare," he said to Hannah as they drove on through Far West. "And I am glad you girls found Sister Williams yesterday. She's a grand old lady and a good friend to have."

Hannah nodded, and Father smiled. "I'd like to introduce you to another very special woman— Mary Fielding Smith."

"The wife of Hyrum Smith?" Hannah breathed.

"Your mother washed up some of your old baby clothes for her," Father explained. "And

I've brought along a few other things I thought she and her new baby could use."

How kind Father is, Hannah thought as they walked up to the door.

"It is for our sakes and the Lord's that the Prophet and his brother are imprisoned," Father explained gently. "It is a privilege for us to be able to be of service to their loved ones left without their care."

The pale woman welcomed them into the humble rooms where she was living. *She could not be more gracious if this were the hall of a splendid palace,* Hannah thought.

Sister Smith was de-
lighted with the things
Father brought, and
Hannah was delighted
with the tiny baby boy
sleeping in a cradle near
their feet. A flush of pleasure lit the mother's fine
oval eyes when she lifted
and examined the small baby clothes. Suddenly Mary turned those soft eyes on Hannah.

"I have heard of what you and your friends did yesterday," she smiled. "Acts of kindness spread a glow that warms many."

Hannah felt her face go pink and warm at the words of praise.

"I am proud of your acts of kindness," Mary Fielding Smith continued, "and of your courage. Your Heavenly Father is pleased with you, Hannah."

"I would like that," Hannah breathed. "I would like to someday be as good as my father and mother are."

"Keep desiring it, and it shall come to pass." Sister Smith leaned forward and planted a kiss on Hannah's cheek. "Is there anything I can do for you?" she asked, and Hannah could feel the warmth of her love reach out to her like a caress.

Hannah found herself telling the quiet woman about Isaac and the death of his mother—and the frightened, confused misery of his father. Mary's eyes filled with tears as she listened. "Let us pray for the poor child and his father," she said. "I am grateful Isaac has your family to take care of him. I am sure with you he will get all of the love he needs."

Hannah and Father walked out into the street, and the sun seemed too glaring, the city walkways too crowded. "It was beautiful in there, wasn't it, Father?" Hannah said, wishing she could explain how she had felt.

"Yes," he replied. "The Spirit of the Lord was in that room, not the spirit of the world. That is why you were loathe to leave it, my dear."

He understands perfectly, Hannah realized, and she thought she knew why. *Part of that spirit he brought with him, in his own heart—and he carries it with him wherever he goes.*

Chapter
Four

A Difficult Decision

They would have to leave Far West and find a new place to live—that much was for certain. Governor Boggs had made it illegal for Mormons to live in the state of Missouri anymore.

"Wherever we are together as a family, that is home," Mother had assured Hannah.

"Wherever the Saints are—that is the home I'm after," Father added with a wink.

"Is it true that a man could shoot a Mormon and it would be legal?" Matthew asked.

Eli nodded grimly. "It's true—if we don't follow the governor's order to leave the state." Seeing the fear in his brother's eyes, he added with a chuckle, "But you needn't worry. None of the mobbers would be interested in a scrawny young specimen like you."

Eli looks more like a man, Hannah thought, watching him, *than a boy who has just turned fifteen. I know he's a great help to Father. I must try to be more help to Mother, since I'm the only daughter she has.*

Thanks to the determination of Brigham Young the Saints were well organized; Hannah knew that. She knew her father was one of some four hundred men who had signed a covenant—a sacred agreement to help the widows and those without money to leave the state, as well as their own families. "Brother Brigham is just trying to remind us that we are brothers and sisters," he explained. "And responsible for one another, before God, our Father."

So the preparations went forth: sewing and mending, canning, preserving—drying fruit and curing meat, what little they had of it.

"We must be ready to leave in February, with the first spring thaws," Father announced.

"Where will we be going?" Benjamin asked.

"Where God directs us," was Father's firm and only reply.

Meanwhile, the autumn colors faded and the berries shriveled on their bushes, and winds from the north, with teeth in them, stripped the land. It had been only two weeks, but Isaac settled into the life of the family. Mother taught him how to say his own name, and the names of the other boys, though Nathaniel was shortened to "Nat" and Benjamin to "Ben," and he called Hannah "Hah-Hah." *Soot* was his favorite word.

"Isaac wants Soot!" he would pout whenever he felt unhappy or thwarted. But he was a bright, cheerful child. Every day Hannah found herself loving him more.

"Please, Heavenly Father," she said every night in her prayers. "Please let Isaac become our little boy. Please don't take him away."

Hannah watched Mother closely. She always seemed tired lately, with worry lines creasing her face. And Hannah overheard her say to Father one evening, "There is too much to care for, too much to do already, Paul. I cannot handle more. Besides, you know how I feel."

Father kissed her and smoothed her damp hair back from her forehead, and appeared very concerned.

Hannah lay awake in her bed that night. *Am I selfish to want to keep Isaac?* she wondered. *But he already seems such a part of us! No one else could love him as we do—no one else could want him as much as I do!*

The next morning she decided that she must approach Mother outright. So, when Isaac fell asleep on the kitchen rug with his arms around Soot, she gathered all her courage together. "Mother, don't you want to keep Isaac?" she said. "Don't you love him, the way I do?"

Mother looked up from her breadboard, her eyes wide with astonishment. "Is that what you have been thinking, my child?"

Hannah nodded, miserable.

"I wouldn't mind the scrimping and sharing—you ought to know that, Hannah—though sometimes I do get discouraged, during the times I'm running thin on faith as well as thin on wheat," she smiled.

"But you love him?"

"I love him," Mother assured her. "You know that already, Hannah."

She was right. Hannah knew. But there was something—she had felt it, she had seen it in Mother's eyes.

"His coming here has made me think of my sister Hannah," Mother confessed, her eyes misting over. "His poor mother dead, unable to know him and raise him. When I think upon it, Hannah, I get the strongest feeling that he is not meant to be ours."

"Of course he is!" Hannah retorted, a panic rising within her. "Look at all the love he has here—and brothers to help him—and—" Tears were choking her voice now.

"It is a feeling of the Spirit I have," Mother said softly, reaching out for her hand. "I want you to pray with me about it, Hannah. Will you do that?"

Hannah pouted for a moment, refusing to answer.

"Pray that the Lord will do that which is best for Isaac—whatever that is."

"I can't!" Hannah protested.

"Yes, you can, my dear," Mother soothed. "You do not want to—that is the problem right now." She turned her head to look at the sleeping child, his hair tumbling like black silk over Soot's white feathers. "But I believe that you love him enough to want, in your heart, what is truly best for him."

There was sadness in Mother's eyes and in her voice. With a start Hannah realized how much

Mother truly loved the little stranger who had come into their lives, and how difficult it was for her to think of letting him go.

"I will try, Mother!" she said. "I promise."

Mother nodded slowly. "I knew you would, Hannah," she said. "I have not forgotten the promise the elders gave me concerning you, and what a joy and blessing you would be in my life."

That night, with Mother's love as her strength, Hannah somehow got down on her knees. For a long time no words would come—only tears and a terrible struggling. Then she found herself speaking to her Heavenly Father with all her heart.

"Thank you for sending Isaac to us to love," she said. "Please take care of him. Do what will make him happy—what is the very best thing for him."

When she crawled into bed she felt peace, as warm as her mother's quilt, spread over her. *Things will be all right,* she thought sleepily. *Heavenly Father will know what is the best thing to do.*

Chapter Five

A FAMILY FOR ISAAC

Mary Fielding Smith at our house! Hannah was too surprised to do anything but stand there and stare.

"Come inside," Mother urged, walking around Hannah to open the door.

"So, this is the child," Sister Smith said. Isaac looked up and smiled at her. "He is very beautiful, isn't he?" She paused a moment, watching him play with the bright spools Benjamin had painted for him and strung on a string. "I believe I have found a mother for him," she said, turning careful eyes on Hannah. "Would you like to hear?"

Hannah nodded, her throat already tightening painfully.

"Please," Mother said.

"There is a young convert family in Far West," Mary began. "They come from a wealthy Boston family who has disowned them because they have joined the Church. They possess very little of the world's goods, but they have been content with the choice they have made." She drew a breath and went on, her voice low and unhurried. "Several months ago the young woman, Esther, gave birth to a child—a little boy who became the light of their lives. Then sickness snatched him away; he died in his sleep. When the mother went to his cradle and drew him into her arms, his spirit was no longer there. Her heart"—Mary's voice faltered—"was nearly broken. But she and her husband did not lose faith. They have been praying that God would send them another child to comfort their hearts."

Silence as sweet as a song hovered in the room when her voice went still. "I know you love Isaac dearly, but I truly believe he is the answer to Esther and Michael's prayers."

"Yes," Hannah sighed. "And I believe they are a very quick answer to mine."

When Sister Smith's eyebrows went up in curiosity it seemed only natural to tell her what had happened. "You see," Mary said softly, "our Father's answer is always consistent—and filled with love for each of us. That is why he whispered what he did to your mother's heart."

"When . . . do you . . ." Hannah began.

"May the Browns come by tonight?"

"By all means," Mother said. "We will look forward to meeting them. Any couple chosen to be the parents of Isaac will be choice people indeed."

Mother washed Isaac's clothes—hand-me-downs from the boys—and hung them out to dry. Hannah gave him a bath, and wound his wet hair round her finger so that it hung in curls down his neck. She sang to him while she worked. Then she whistled for Soot, and the three of them went for a walk—one last walk around the farm they would soon leave forever, the land Father had cleared and planted and hoped to harvest for the rest of his life.

"We cannot always plan," she told Isaac. "For only God sees the future. We are all in his hands. If we let him, he will make us happy. That's what he is doing for you."

She knelt down beside him so that their eyes met. "Please don't forget us," she pleaded. "I will never forget you. Even when I am grown-up with little boys of my own—even when I am a wrinkled old lady, I will pray for you, Isaac, every day of my life."

She drew him close to her. He smelled of soap and goose down. He cuddled his damp little head against her shoulder. After a very long time she released him. "We'd better go back now," she said, reaching down for his hand. He slipped it into hers—so small, so warm against her palm—and they walked back to the house, Soot waddling behind, being amazingly quiet and docile as if he, too, knew what was about to take place.

Hannah was at the door emptying the dishpan when Esther and Michael Brown started up the path to the house. She watched them: the rhythm of their walk and the faint sound of their voices carried over the thin autumn air. As they drew closer the young woman reached for her husband's hand. *She is afraid,* Hannah realized. She hurried back to put away the unsightly dishpan

41

and tell Mother that they were coming. Then, not knowing exactly why, she stepped back outside.

The man and woman were nearly at the porch now. Hannah caught her breath when she saw that Esther's hair was violet black, like a raven's wing, and her eyes were as blue as the sky.

"Come in!" Hannah cried. "We've been waiting for you." From her heart she sent up a silent plea: *Let Isaac like her. Let him go to her, Heavenly Father, and not be afraid.*

Esther smiled shyly. "You are so kind to let us come," she murmured.

Hannah held the door open wide, and Mother urged them inside. When Esther saw Isaac she made a little gasping sound and put her hand to her mouth.

"He's beautiful, isn't he?" Mother said softly. "And, my goodness, he looks just like you."

Isaac heard and glanced up from his play. His eyes traveled the circle and came to rest on the face of the lovely young woman, who tried to smile through her tears.

"Isaac." She spoke only his name, and then held out her arms. He hesitated a moment, and she stretched her arms further, beseeching. He went. The two dark heads mingled as she drew him into her gentle embrace.

Much later, when the Browns took their reluctant leave, it seemed to Hannah that she had known Esther and Michael for years.

"We'll bring him to visit often," Esther promised, her eyes shining.

"And remember that I'll watch him for you," Hannah responded, "whenever you need."

"The boys and I will be over next week to help you with that wagon box," Father said. "And, if you'd like, you may as well plan right now to travel with us."

Back and forth, back and forth they went, warm and friendly, and not anxious to part. Esther crept close to Mother. "Please," she began hesitantly. "Michael and I have no one; our families are far away, and lost to us. So, you see, we don't want to take Isaac from you. We hope . . ."

Mother put her arm around the young, trembling woman. "Bless you," she said. "We need one another, and that is as it should be."

"Grandparents," Hannah laughed. "Mother and Father will be Isaac's grandparents—and we'll be aunt and uncles to him."

"And to all the rest of your children," Mother added.

"It is too much to hope for," Esther whispered.

"No," Mother said with gentle firmness. "We shall bless one another, as Heavenly Father intended, and make a family carved out of love."

And perhaps, Hannah thought, *up in heaven Isaac's mother will find a way to care for the little child Esther lost.*

"This is the gospel of love," Father had often told her. Watching the faces around her, feeling the wonder and joy flow through her, Hannah understood what he meant—and she knew she would cherish that understanding and knowledge for the rest of her life.

HIGHLIGHTS FROM HISTORY

Missouri
1831–1839

In the spring and summer of 1831 many important revelations were given to the Prophet Joseph, among them Doctrine and Covenants 57, which designated Jackson County, Missouri, as Zion—"the land which I have appointed and consecrated for the gathering of the saints. . . . This is the land of promise, and the place for the city of Zion." (D&C 57:1, 2.) The Saints purchased land as the Lord instructed them, and the Prophet dedicated it as a gathering place.

The city of Independence, or Zion (meaning "the pure in heart"), was laid out foursquare like the New Jerusalem spoken of in the book of Revelation, with the streets wide and crossing one another at right angles and each home having enough ground for lawns in front and gardens in back. Barns and outbuildings were to be erected outside the city, so as not to mar the beauty and order of the whole. This "city of Zion" plan was later instituted both in Nauvoo and Salt Lake.

Joseph liked the looks of the country around Independence: large rolling prairies sprinkled with wildflowers; rich soil; timber along the watercourses; a climate mild and pleasant most of the year. He was not so pleased with the degraded, benighted nature of most of the people who lived in the region—in his own words, the "leanness of intellect, ferocity, and jealousy of a people that were nearly a century behind the times."

The Colesville Branch moved to that location "en masse," and, under the direction of Bishop Edward Partridge, the members were challenged to live the law of consecration and to purchase lands as quickly as possible for the inheritance of the Saints. *The Evening and the Morning Star,* the first periodical of the Church, was established, and a branch of the Gilbert and Whitney store opened in Independence. By the end of 1831 there were branches of the Church in twenty states and in parts of Canada. By the middle of 1833 between twelve and fifteen thousand Saints had "gathered" to Jackson County, Missouri.

Most of the Missourians were from the South; most of the early converts to Mormonism, from the eastern states. There was conflict over politics, the slave issue, the strength of numbers and organization which was obvious among the Mormons, and the "strangeness" of Latter-day Saint religious beliefs. On July 20, 1833, a council of those opposed to the Mormons (between four and five hundred men) met at the Independence courthouse and determined ways to get rid of these people "peaceably if we can, forcibly if we must." Encouraging one another, they decided that they could not wait for the "delays incident to legislation," but drew up their own arbitrary list of demands, which stipulated that no more Mormons should move into the area, that those now there pledge to remove themselves within a reasonable time, that the editor of the *Star* close up his printing, and that an ill fate would await those who failed to comply.

They presented their preposterous demands to the Saints, who begged the space of three months to consider, but were denied that and a subsequent plea for ten days; at last they were afforded fifteen minutes to either accept or reject. According to their own pleasure, then, this mob of men began to wreck, despoil, and drive the helpless Mormons from their homes. The stunned and terrified people were forced to seek refuge in neighboring counties, especially Clay

County to the north. They were denied aid by Governor Dunklin, and many of the leaders of the mob held high government and judicial positions as judges, postmasters, constables, and city clerks. Joseph wept when he heard of the fate of his people, and organized Zion's Camp to march to their aid, though the learning and training experience of the men involved in the camp achieved more lasting benefit for the Church than did any overt help the men were able to offer their suffering brethren.

Following the completion of the temple in Kirtland, Joseph and the majority of the Saints there removed to Missouri—over sixteen hundred during the first seven months of 1838. Meanwhile, the Mormons in Clay County had apparently outstayed their welcome, and agreed to settle northeast of there in the wild, desolate prairie regions of Ray County, the first settlers pitching their tents on Shoal Creek—later to be named, as a settlement, Far West. Joseph, concerned about finding places for all his people to live, selected sites for other settlements, including Spring City, which the Saints called Di-Ahman because it was revealed to the Prophet that this was Adam-ondi-Ahman, the place where Adam had blessed his posterity and where he would one day come to visit his people. At the request of

Far West, Missouri

Mormon leaders, two new counties—Caldwell and Daviess—were created out of northern Ray County; in this area the people pouring in could make their homes.

But peace, after the Saints' faith and their efforts, was not to be. Spurred by an incident at the election polls in Gallatin in August 1838, the mobbers came out more openly and ferociously against the Saints, until in October, with the force of a thunderbolt striking from a clear sky, came Governor Boggs's legal order that the Mormons were to be "exterminated or driven from the state."

The Saints moved cautiously; but the state was flooded with lies concerning them. The outlying settlements were attacked: DeWitt, and then Haun's Mill, where men and boys were mercilessly killed, children's brains blown out with malice and glee, and one sixty-two-year-old man shot with his own gun and then hacked to pieces.

An army of two thousand bloodthirsty men gathered around Far West, which by this time had grown to a population of nearly five thousand inhabitants, now virtually helpless to defend themselves. The mob's first victory was the surrender, by treachery, of the Prophet Joseph, his brother Hyrum, and other leaders, who were intended to be shot the following morning in the public square. But Brigadier General Alexander Doniphan, who had received Major General Samuel Lucas's orders, flatly refused. "It is cold-blooded murder," he replied. "I will not obey your order. . . . And if you execute these men, I will hold you responsible before an earthly tribunal, so help me God." The mob was let loose to despoil and terrorize the city. Joseph and his brethren were marched to Independence, transferred to Richmond, and then imprisoned for months in Liberty Jail, where the choice revelations recorded in sections 121 and 122 of the Doctrine and Covenants were given to the Prophet in his hour of need.

Under the dedicated and inspired leadership of Brigham Young, the Saints abandoned their homes and belongings and walked—through rain, mud, and snow—from the state. Many gathered at Quincy, Illinois, where they were kindly received, or huddled on the Iowa shore of the Mississippi until some provision for their future homes could be made.

In April 1839, Joseph and his brethren were allowed to escape, rejoining the Saints in Quincy on the twenty-second of that month. Two days later a council meeting empowered a committee to travel north "for the purpose of making a location for the Church." A place called Commerce—situated on a gentle horseshoe bend, half-encircled by the wide Mississippi—was chosen as the central gathering place. Joseph felt that here, with "the blessing of heaven," the Saints could build a city, and he renamed the spot Nauvoo, a Hebrew word signifying "a beautiful situation, or place, carrying with it, also, the idea of rest."

About the Author

Susan Evans McCloud is the author of over thirty books. Those for children include *A. A. Seagull, I'm Going to Be Baptized, Black Stars over Mexico,* and *Jennie.* Mrs. McCloud has also written newspaper feature articles, scripts for filmstrips, screenplays, and lyrics—including two hymns for the 1985 Church hymnal. She is a part-time teacher of English and creative writing, and is a tour guide at Brigham Young's Beehive House. She and her husband, James, are the parents of six children, and the grandparents of four. Mrs. McCloud loves history, poetry, travel, flowers, Scottish music, and "tea" parties.

About the Artist

In addition to the pictures found in this book, Jessica Mormann Chopelas has drawn those found in the other books about Hannah—*New Friends* and *A Lesson Learned*—as well as the books in the *Sophie, a Kirtland Girl* series. She has also done the artwork for a book about baptism called *What Is White?* Mrs. Chopelas lives in Massachusetts with her husband, Karl, and their two children, Alexander and Julia. She enjoys the timeless crafts of bookbinding by hand, cultivating herbs, and processing sheep's wool. With Alex and Julia, Mrs. Chopelas loves to walk on the beach, read books, and visit farms.